Some of the Adventures of

RHODE ISLAND RED

by Stephen Manes

Illustrated by William Joyce

HarperTrophy

A Division of HarperCollinsPublishers

Library of Congress Cataloging-in-Publication Data
Manes, Stephen, 1949–
   Some of the adventures of Rhode Island Red / by Stephen Manes ;
illustrated by William Joyce.
      p.   cm.
   Summary: A diminutive red-haired man no bigger than a hen's egg,
Rhode Island Red leaves his home among the chickens and travels
throughout Rhode Island, becoming a legendary figure through his many
heroic exploits..
   ISBN 0-397-32347-6. — ISBN 0-397-32348-4 (lib. bdg.)
   ISBN 0-06-440358-0 (pbk.)
   [1. Chickens—Fiction   2. Rhode Island—Fiction   3. Tall tales.]
I. Joyce, William, Ill.   II. Title.
PZ7.M31264So   1990   89-35397
[Fic]—dc20   CIP
                                                            AC

First Harper Trophy edition, 1993.

for Susan,
with cluck

CONTENTS

Some of the Adventures of

RHODE ISLAND RED

Rhode Island may be the tiniest state in the union, but that doesn't mean it's a sissy. Take the weather up there: It can come down on you quicker than a hungry mosquito and twice as mean.

And I know what I'm talking about. One summer evening east of Usquepaugh, I was driving under skies as blue as the hero's eyes. Next thing I knew, it was black as the bad guy's hat and wet as the heroine's cheeks. Through the sheets of rain, I could make out a dim light a ways off in the distance. I just missed losing the narrow road seven times or eight, but finally I made it to an old farmhouse.

I went to the door and knocked. A thousand chickens cackled wildly in the farmyard. It brought to mind what my Uncle Lyndon always used to say: "Only thing madder than a wet hen is five hundred of 'em."

And that's when a grizzled old farmer opened the door and pointed a long shotgun at my middle. "What's your business, mister?" he inquired.

"It's pouring out here," I replied, politely touching my fingertips to the brim of my Stetson. "May I come in?"

The farmer lowered his weapon. "What're you doing up here in this part of the country, cowboy?" he asked. I guess he must've noticed my filigreed boots.

"I'm researching a magazine story about the back roads and byways of Rhode Island," I said sincerely. "Won't be much to write about if I can't see 'em for all this rain."

"A writer, eh?" said the farmer. "Well, take off that forty-quart chapeau and come on in."

Suddenly the bloodcurdling crow of what sounded

like a thirty-foot rooster rose above the rain and thunder. It set me shivering.

"What in the name of Sam Houston was that?" I asked.

"Why, that's Rhode Island Red," said the farmer.

I stepped through the doorway. "One of your chickens?"

"Chicken?" shouted the farmer in outrage. "Chicken? He's no chicken! I'm talking about Rhode Island Red! Biggest hero we ever had around here!"

"Never heard of him," I said.

"Never heard of him!" The farmer cocked his gun and looked as though he'd shoot me on the spot. "Never heard of him? Where you from, ignoramus?"

"Texas," I stammered.

"Texas!" he exclaimed, shaking his head. "A big shot from the Lone Star State! I might've known it!" He looked madder than ever, but he lowered the shotgun.

"Listen, pardner," he went on in the world's worst

imitation of a Texan, "I'll bet you've heard of Pecos Bill, toughest critter west of the Alamo."

"Naturally," I replied.

"And Paul Bunyan, the man mountain lumberjack."

"Sure."

"And John Henry, the human dynamo of a steel driver."

"Of course."

"Well, Rhode Island Red could best any man of 'em. Why, he could outrassle any *two* of 'em. In fact, if he set his mind to it, he could whip the three of 'em put together. Did, once."

I made a face. "If this guy is everything you say, how come I've never heard of him?"

"I'll tell you why. Because there's just one thing those other fellows had that he didn't."

"And what was that?"

"A biographer! Heck, Red's so famous around here, nobody ever bothered to set down his life story." The farmer gave me a curious look. "Say, you claim you're a writer. Maybe you'd like the honor."

"Perhaps some other time," I replied. I had places to go. People to see. Things to do. Last thing I needed was to get trapped into listening to some cock-and-bull story.

The farmer raised his shotgun again. "Friend, I'm sick and tired of meeting up with foreigners like yourself who know every battle all those other heroes ever fought and what they ate for breakfast, but don't know thing number one about Rhode Island Red, the greatest of them all. Now, either you start writing or I start shooting."

I whipped out my notebook and sat down in a big old chair.

"If I go too fast for you, you just say so," the farmer ordered. "You take it down just like I tell it. Every single word."

Again that unearthly crowing cut through the

night like a rifle shot. "Red approves of you," the farmer said with a grin. Then he leaned back in his rocker and commenced his tale.

CHAPTER ONE
RED IS FOUND

This here's the story of Rhode Island Red. A tougher little bantamweight you never heard of, who feared neither man nor beast. He could lick a fellow twenty times his size before breakfast and then rassle bears till lunch. But I'm getting ahead of myself.

The first anybody ever heard of Red was when they found him in Mrs. Huckaby's henhouse. The Mrs. was gathering eggs, and when she stuck her hand under Old Rhody, the queen of the flock, she felt something soft and squishy-like. Mrs. Huckaby squeezed her hand around it, and all of a sudden there was a yell so bloodcurdling it fractured her spectacles.

Well, Mrs. H. was pretty nearsighted, so she had to move Rhody aside and squat down real close to the nest to see what was making all that commotion. She could see a broken egg, but Mrs. H. never heard of a broken egg hollering like that. So she looked a little closer.

There in the middle of the yolk was a little baby boy no bigger than your toenail and nearly as pink, wearing a tiny little diaper and kicking like the hind end of a mule. But every time Mrs. Huckaby tried to pick him up, Old Rhody pecked her hand. That hen thought the little fellow was one of her chicks, and nobody could tell her any different.

Now, Mrs. H. knew Rhody was the best mother anybody could ask for. The short of it is, Mr. and Mrs. H. decided to let Rhody raise the tad till he outgrew the nest. They named him Red, and they treated him like the son they never had.

Well, Old Rhody loved that funny-looking new-comer as much as any of her others. He was a sturdy little cockerel from the very first, and he shot right to the top of the pecking order. Pushed the other chicks aside and made 'em wait till he was done eating, no matter how much they flapped their wings, he did.

Sure, he was a little different from the rest, but to Rhody that made him special. She didn't mind that he wasn't fluffy at first and didn't grow feathers later, or a comb. Or that he never got much bigger than egg-size. In fact, she was proud of his differences—especially that carrot-colored fuzz on the top of his head.

Rhody brought Red up the very best she could. It took her quite a time to get him off all fours and up on two legs the way chicks are supposed to do. And he always spoke chicken with a smidgen of human accent. But he was a pretty fast learner and generally one step ahead of the other chicks his age. Not a one could beat him to the first kernel of corn in the morning, and not a one could best him in a fight. Old Rhody was quietly proud.

And so were Mr. and Mrs. Huckaby. Every morning when the sun came up, their boy'd perch on the fence rail and cock-a-doodle-doo loud enough to wake the entire state and parts of Connecticut. Course, when he spoke New England, it was with a slight poultry accent, but the Huckabys figured he'd outgrow that.

He did, too. What he never outgrew was the other chickens. True enough, he was a mite on the runty side to start with, but Mr. and Mrs. H. always expected one day he'd shoot up like spring corn.

Never happened. Time he was due to get himself an education, he'd been egg-size nearly seven years. Mr. and Mrs. H. worried a little, but the law said he had to go to school, so off to school he went.

The first boy he met on the way thought Red looked a little puny to get an education. "Where you goin', little fella?" he asked.

"School," Red replied.

"School's for big kids," said the boy, kicking Red aside. "Go on home, runt!"

Well, he shouldn't ought've done that. It got Red so mad he jumped on that boy and clawed and scratched and pecked him till he begged for mercy. Red made him trade lunches before he let him up. And when that bully saw what he got for his trade, he knew he was whipped for fair. He said he couldn't possibly get through the day on just a handful of corn, but Red told him to quit complaining or he'd show him a thing or five.

The next person they met up with was a fat girl. That boy warned her not to tangle with Red, but she couldn't believe such a little pipsqueak could harm her. Of course, before she knew it, she was flat on her back, apologizing and handing over *her* lunch; this time, Red didn't even offer to trade. By noontime, the little fellow had enough lunches to last your average person a week. He'd beaten up ten kids and an English teacher—which was not really something to crow about.

"Now just what did you do to Mr. Loggins, little fellow?" asked the principal when Red turned up in her office. But by now he was very sensitive to remarks about his size. Before she could get another word in edgewise, he'd clawed her beautiful first-day-of-school dress to ribbons, which was not a very herolike thing to do.

"Go straight home, you little demon!" the principal shrieked. "And don't come back till you learn how to behave like a human being!" She pinned an angry note to his shirt and escorted him out the door.

Well, Mr. and Mrs. Huckaby never did get that note. It was considerably bigger than Red was, and on the way home he tripped over it so many times he tore it up and made spitballs out of it.

"School's out for the year," he told Mr. and Mrs. H. when they wondered why he was home so early, and since Red always told the truth as he saw it, they had no reason to doubt him. And Red didn't think he ought to mention all those lunches of his when Mrs. Huckaby asked him why he was just pecking at his dinner. He just told her he had a little bellyache. It wasn't really a fib.

It was quite a time before the principal felt brave enough to venture down to the Huckaby farm. When she noticed Red out in the farmyard, scrabbling for his breakfast with the chickens, she had an inkling the boy was a trifle unusual. After Mr. and Mrs. H. explained the particulars of Red's young life, the principal told them Red simply wasn't fit to go to school—and he wouldn't be, either, unless he learned the social graces. She recommended they send him to Professor Wigglesworth, the local professor of etiquette.

Well, Mr. Wigglesworth had seen some tough cases in his time, but never one quite as bad as Red. Seemed like Red didn't do anything the way normal folk did. When the Professor first laid eyes on him, the lad was strutting around the room and crowing like the cock of the walk. When the Professor extended his hand, Red didn't shake it—he just pecked it hard. It was quite a challenge for the Professor, but he rose to the occasion and said he'd give it a try, though he'd have to charge twice his usual fee because of the difficulty of the case.

Mr. Huckaby was kind of put out about that. Considering Red's size, he thought he'd be eligible for a discount. But finally he said okay.

The first thing the Professor did was sit Red down on top of eight or ten phone books at the dinner table. Mrs. Wigglesworth brought them both steaming bowls of chowder.

"Now, then," the Professor began, "which utensil would you use for this dish?" But even before he could finish asking the question, Red was pecking away at his bowl, slurping like a sump pump. He sprayed soup all over himself, the tablecloth, and Professor Wigglesworth.

"Young man," said the Professor sadly, wiping his face as Red pecked at a slippery clam, "I am afraid there is nothing I can do for you."

So Red's academic career was doomed from the first. Mr. and Mrs. Huckaby were very disappointed. They had high hopes that their son might go into medicine, since he could ask people to say "Ah" and then slip right down their gullet to see what was bothering 'em. Or maybe he'd take up the law, seeing as how the fine print that mystified most folks was headline-size to him. Alas, the Huckabys had to abandon those dreams for their boy.

But just because a person ain't educated don't mean he don't know nothin'. Red stayed home and learned pretty near everything there was to learn about the farm by helping the Huckabys. And he mellowed out a little as he grew up—well, as he grew older, 'cause up is one thing he never did grow.

Anyhow, it was a good life for him, and he appreciated it. But like all heroes, Red got a hankering to wander—that itch to seek his fame and fortune. And when you're a hero and you get that itch, not even a bad head cold can stop it. The Huckabys wept and pleaded with him not to go, and Old Rhody begged him to stay, but Red's little mind was all made up. He wrapped a few kernels of corn in an old eye patch, slung it over his shoulder, bid his friends good-bye, and set off across the rolling hills. The Huckabys gave him a dime as a going-away present.

"You don't believe me," said the farmer, leaning toward that shotgun.

"Did I say anything of the kind?" I demanded.

"You frowned it."

"I frowned because I'm down to the end of my notepad."

"Got it all down? Want me to repeat anything?"

"I've got every word," I said. I'd been writing so furiously my hand had cramped up. "I do need some more paper," I added, trying to shake some life into my paw.

The old farmer rooted around in a big rolltop desk and handed me a five-year-old calendar with pictures of comely hens in provocative poses. "You can write on the back," he said. "Now where was I?"

"Red had set out to seek his fame and fortune," I sighed.

"Right. Let's see, now . . ."

CHAPTER TWO

RED AND THE SKINNY CHICKENS

Now, everything's relative. What you—

"Wait a second!" shouted the farmer, looking closely at the calendar. "Why, this'n'll be back in season next year."

He snatched the calendar from my lap, tossed it back inside the desk, and handed me an old newspaper. "Write in the margins," he commanded. "Now, where was I . . . ? As I was saying . . ."

CHAPTER TWO

RED AND THE SKINNY CHICKENS

Now, everything's relative. What you might consider just a short stretch of the legs was quite a long haul for a fellow Red's size. By the end of the morning, he still hadn't even crossed the Huckabys' property line, and at that rate, he'd never get much wandering done. Lucky for Red, a friendly box turtle ambled past around lunchtime and offered him a lift. By the end of the day, they'd gone nearly a mile, which when you stop to consider it is biting off a pretty good hunk of this fair state of ours.

Around evening, they rode up near a farmyard. Red thanked the turtle, pointed him in the direction of a nearby creek, and headed straight for the chicken coop. It wasn't that Red didn't care for humans, mind you; he just tended to find poultry better company. They weren't always worrying about mortgages and dentists and shining their shoes and stuff like that.

Even from a distance, Red's eagle eye noticed this flock looked a little scrawny. But the minute he strutted in, the top cock strutted up and demanded to know who he was.

"Name's Red," came the reply in perfect chicken. "Who might you be?"

"Now, just one minute, stranger," said Big Tom. "Are you chicken or human?"

"A little of both, I s'pose," Red said.

"We don't care much for humans 'round here."

"Then consider me fowl."

"Where are your feathers?"

"Plucked," Red replied.

"Well, you must be one of us, all right. Never knew any human to speak chicken. Come on in."

Big Tom introduced himself and announced the visitor to the rest of the flock. They converged on Red as if he were a morsel of feed. He was such an odd-looking creature that they all wanted to hear his life story.

And he'd've been delighted to oblige them, but before he could get started, a handful of corn pelted down from above. The whole flock screamed and hollered and fought and scrambled for it. In about eight seconds, the corn'd disappeared, but every last chicken was still hungry.

"Kind of him to serve an appetizer," said Red. "Where I come from, you get your dinner all at once."

"Appetizer!" Big Tom snorted. "That *was* our dinner!"

"You mean to say he feeds this whole flock one measly handful of corn?"

"You saw it with your own baby blues. Whenever there's an economy move, us chickens are the first to feel the pinch. Why, half the time that old buzzard gets drunk and forgets to feed us at all."

"Why don't you organize?" asked Red.

"A lot of good that would do!" huffed one bony hen.

"Go on strike!" Red continued. "Refuse to lay any more eggs till he feeds you a decent ration."

"Ha!" clucked Big Tom. "One eggless day, and we'd all be chicken soup."

"Use your noodle, chicken!" Red exploded. "Why, you're all so skinny, he'd be lucky to get one cup of broth out of the whole flock of you. Besides, you've got one thing now you never had before."

"What's that?"

"An interpreter. Someone who can translate your demands into human lingo."

"Who?"

"At your service." Red bowed.

Big Tom didn't buy it. "Now, just a minute, stranger. This is getting pretty farfetched. I never heard of any chicken talking human."

Red started in again on his life story by way of explanation. But before he could get three words out, the farmer came back again, weaving tipsily and waving his salt shaker at the tails of likely-looking fryers.

The only one who didn't scurry out of the way was Red. He grabbed the farmer's pant cuff, tugged hard, and brought him down to the chicken-coop floor with a thud.

"Consarn the blankety-dab fowl anyway," rumbled the farmer. He was about to get up when he saw a tiny figure of a man appear before his eyes.

"Now look here," said the red-haired apparition, speaking human lingo. "I won't let you treat these chickens this way."

The farmer shook his head back and forth and slapped himself hard. Either he was drunk beyond hope or he'd fallen into a den of leprechauns. "Who are you?" he asked.

"Rhode Island Red," said the proud little fellow with his hands on his hips. "And I won't let you treat my friends this way."

"I'm drunk for fair," said the farmer. He laid his head down and fell asleep right there on the chicken-coop floor.

Next morning, the farmer woke up to find himself surrounded by chickens. Chickens to the right of him, chickens to the left of him, chickens on top of him, chickens all over him. He raised his hand to swat them out of the way, but some mysterious force held his arm so he couldn't move it.

"I wouldn't do that if I were you," said a voice beside his ear.

The farmer turned his head and saw a little red-haired fellow with muscles like pine knots. "Seems like I've met up with you before," said the farmer, "though I can't recollect the name."

"Rhode Island Red," said the little man.

"A fowl name if ever there was one," replied the farmer. "What are all these dadblasted chickens doing all over me, anyhow?"

"Making their grievances heard," said Red. "They're

tired of short rations and contemptible mistreatment. They're united in a common cause—namely, to get a decent wage for themselves and their loved ones."

Where Red had learned such highfalutin language I have no idea. Anyhow, the farmer asked him what would happen if he refused their demands.

"No more eggs," said Red. "And you may find most of your employees will have flown the coop."

"What's your interest in all this?" the farmer asked.

"Sir," Red said grandly, "my stepmother was a chicken. She plucked me from the lowest depths anyone could imagine. She gave me a home when no one else would bother. Chickens are brother and sister to me."

A tear rolled down the farmer's cheek. "Do you speak chicken?" he asked with a hitch in his voice.

"Fluently," Red replied.

"Then tell these birds I apologize. Tell them they'll have a double ration of corn from now on. Tell them they needn't fear the cookpot till they're too old to care. And tell them that from this day forward I will never take another sip of whiskey."

Red translated the farmer's pledge, and the chickens cheered wildly. Big Tom strutted up to the farmer and pecked him on the nose.

"Now, what was that all about?" asked the farmer.

"A thank-you kiss," Red replied.

"Well, I'll be swoggled," said the farmer, rising to his feet.

It was quite a beginning to Red's career as a hero. The chickens gave him four clucks—the fowl version of three cheers. They hoisted him onto their shoulders. They paraded him all around the henhouse.

And as for the farmer, he was as good as his word. From that day on, those chickens were the best-kept and best-fed fowl in all New England. The hens won so many blue ribbons they sewed 'em into babushkas, and the roosters used their prizes for neckties.

"Another frown!" barked the farmer.

"My forehead was itchy," I replied.

"Then scratch it! Quit interrupting!"

I scratched. "Just for the record, did the farmer keep his word?"

"I certainly did."

"You!" I scoffed. "You don't mean to tell me *you* were that farmer!"

"Who else? I wouldn't tell you a story I couldn't personally vouch for."

"But you've been drinking ever since I came in here."

"Purest rainwater," said the farmer. "Purest rainwater."

"I see," I said, though it certainly didn't look or smell like that to me. I scowled, trying to think of a way to escape this crackpot. But it was impossible. The rain was pounding like cannonballs on the roof.

"Now, don't go breaking in again," the farmer insisted. "Let me go on with this biography. Take down everything!"

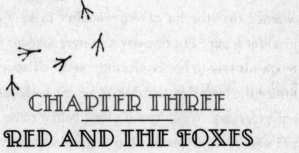

CHAPTER THREE
RED AND THE FOXES

If I do say so, that farmer turned into one of the finest people you'd ever hope to know. Red thought so, too, and he stuck around and took care of some odd jobs that needed doing, like scraping out the drainpipe under the kitchen sink and climbing up behind the pantry to serve an eviction notice on a family of mice that ate rodent poison like it was potato chips. Red got a regular wage of a dime a day, same as all the other hired help. At night he slept in the henhouse. Liked it that way.

Now, the foxes in the area—red ones they were— never did pay much attention to the chickens on this farm. Until Red showed up, those birds were all so wizened that the lot of 'em wouldn't make a decent meal for a pup. But one day a hungry fox was passing by on his way to better pickings, and he happened to notice the birds'd fattened up some. So he kept an eye out every day. Well, 'twasn't long before those chickens were the choicest fowl in the entire state. So Old Foxy decided to drop in sometime and take home a midnight snack.

Now, that fox was pretty quiet as he snuck under the chicken wire. The entire flock was asleep for the night, and not a one of 'em woke up. But Red had the ears of a basset hound, and he thought he heard something a little strange outside.

He crept out of his nest to investigate. He peeked around the henhouse door. Sure enough, two gleaming eyes stared back at him.

Now, this fox'd had a number of dealings with human folk, but this was the very first time he'd seen one smaller than he was. He punched himself in the nose to make sure he wasn't dreaming. Then he asked Red who he was.

Red didn't understand fox lingo, but he kind of guessed what the fox was after, and he clucked out his name. Well, the fox had never seen anything like it: Here was some sixteenth-pint human cackling like a goofy rooster. The fox doubled over with laughter, and while he was hooting and guffawing, he got to wondering what a tender little red-haired human tasted like. Might be the perfect between-meal treat, for all he knew. So Fox stopped laughing and gobbled Red right up into his mouth.

He was just about to start chewing when he felt his jaws snap open from inside. Then he heard a cock-a-doodle-doo so loud he had to hold his ears, and the next thing he knew, the whole farmyard came to life. The chickens were shrieking, and Red was tying Fox's tail in a granny knot, and the farmer came running with his shotgun, and it was all that Fox could do to hightail it back under the chicken wire in one piece. Naturally, Red got his four clucks and his hero's parade again, and the chickens nearly wore him out with admiration.

The local foxes didn't feel quite the same way. In fact, at first most of them didn't believe such a critter as Red even existed. They figured the first fox just invented the story to spare himself some embarrassment over getting bested by some banty rooster. But they decided to check into the matter, and now and then they'd catch a glimpse of Red slopping the hogs or currying the horses or chopping the firewood, so they got the picture that Red was for real.

The foxes wondered what to do. They could've had just about any chicken in the state, but nowadays plain old regular birds just didn't seem worth bothering with. Right here under their noses were a whole bunch of fat, tender, succulent fowl, eating like till they'd burst. The foxes just couldn't rest till they'd sampled 'em. Only trouble was that wiry little fellow those birds had for a guard.

The foxes put their heads together and decided to launch a surprise attack the next stormy night. They figured the rain and the thunder'd cover up any noise they made getting to the chicken coop, along with any hollering the poultry did when they found invaders in their midst. A couple of the bigger guys would gang up on Red, and then the whole flock would be at their mercy.

Well, there were a few things their plan didn't take into account. Now, it may have been tiny, but Red's was the most powerful nose in the history of human existence. When he tuned it in just right, he could tell you from where you're sitting whether my uncle up in Boston was having sausage for breakfast, or bacon. He could tell you exactly what kind of flower bed a passing bee had just come back from, he could tell you in the morning if the governor'd had baked beans for dinner the night before, and he could follow a trail so far it broke many a bloodhound's heart. So when that pack of foxes was headed his way, his nose gave him plenty of advance warning. All he had to do was figure out the best way to stop 'em.

Course, the best way to stop 'em would've been to wake the farmer and have him stand guard with his shotgun. But Red didn't think that would be quite sporting, and being a considerate sort, he didn't want to roust the farmer from his sleep if he didn't have to. Red could've stopped any ten of those foxes single-handed, but he smelled more like a couple dozen on their way, and he was afraid two or three of 'em might snatch themselves some dinner while he was working on the others. Besides, Red always liked to flex his brain rather than his muscles, and since his mind was nearly as sensitive as his nose, it wasn't long before he had a plan.

The twenty-four foxes prepared their assault. Six at the north, six at the east, six at the south, and six where you already figured by now, they dug under the chicken wire and awaited their leader's howl. But over the pouring rain, they suddenly heard an eerie voice clucking what sounded like "The Star-Spangled Banner."

Now, the foxes didn't know chicken, but they knew music. They may've had a lot of bad traits, but they were as patriotic as the next Rhode Islander. They stood on their hind legs, clapped their paws to their hearts, and listened reverently to all four verses of our national anthem. But when the singing stopped, the foxes fell smack on their faces. All their legs were bound together with chicken wire. They were so intent on behaving like model citizens during the song that they didn't notice till too late.

The foxes were furious. "You've used our patriotism to trick us!" cried their leader.

"It's not the first time in history it's happened, foxes, and it won't be the last!" shouted Red in their language. He'd learned it one afternoon from a toothless old vixen who didn't have anything better to do than gab.

Big Tom trained a flashlight on Red as he stood atop the henhouse. "Foxes," Red declared, "we applaud your patriotism. But patriotism must go hand in hand with tolerance. We fowl"—the chickens beamed to hear Red include himself among them—"have a right to live our lives in peace. Why don't you join us and become vegetarians?"

"We'll gladly do that, fellow speaker of fox," shouted the foxes' wily leader. "Merely set us free."

"Certainly," Red answered. "But first our roosters will pass among you with some fine corn to seal the bargain."

The foxes knew they didn't have any choice but to

eat what the chickens set before them. And the foxes didn't enjoy it, either. They grumbled to themselves as they pecked listlessly at the corn.

"Delicious!" proclaimed their leader unconvincingly when he was done. "You've made believers of us! Now set us free!"

"Of course," Red replied. But first the roosters and hens rolled the foxes over and over until even their eyebrows were caked with mud, and you could hardly tell whether they were foxes or rocks or just what. Then Red ordered the chickens back inside the coop, and he untied the foxes' filthy leader.

"We could've called the farmer and had him bring his shotgun," Red told him, "but we didn't. Now you've been warned. If you come around here again, you'll get a lot more than corn and mud for your troubles. Untie your friends, and don't come bothering us anymore."

And that's exactly what the foxes did. Except they weren't red anymore. Nobody really knows whether it was the mud, or the embarrassment, or the scare Red put in 'em, or the combination put all together, but anyhow, every last one turned gray. And they were so fed up with chickens that they and all their relatives left the state entirely. Whenever anybody runs across a red fox in Rhode Island these days, it's bound to be a foolish stray from Connecticut or Massachusetts.

Last I heard, the Rhode Island foxes were out in Iowa. Seems they're at the cornfields all summer long. Only thing that'll keep 'em away is what they call a "scarefox": a little stuffed shirt and a cornhusk head with some carrot curls for hair. It just won't work without the carrot curls, so they tell me. Nor if it's even the slightest bit bigger than a grade-A jumbo egg.

"Now what's the matter with you?" asked the farmer.

I was coughing like a wounded coyote. "Must've caught cold," I rasped.

"This'll fix you right up," he said, pouring something into a tumbler. "Best thing you can do for a cough."

"Much obliged," I said, and drained it dry.

"Purest rainwater," he replied as he bent over and poured me another draft, "with a little something extra." His breath smelled like the wrong end of a glue factory.

"Sip this while you scribble," he said. "And don't you dare interrupt me again."

CHAPTER FOUR
RED SEEKS HIS FORTUNE

Now, eventually Red decided it'd be best to move on again. One story says it was because his boss wouldn't raise his pay to eleven cents per diem, but I can assure you that's pure unadulterated fiction. True, a nickel extra a week's quite a tidy sum, and it might've upset the other hands to see the little fellow promoted faster than they were, but Red would've probably been worth every penny, almost. No, the real reason he left was that his old hero's itch erupted again worse than a dose of the chicken pox.

Big Tom didn't like it one bit. Pleaded with Red, coaxed him, got mad at him, pecked him in the shins, but no matter what he did, he couldn't convince his friend to stay. So when Red went out the farmhouse gate with his traveling gear slung over his shoulder, Big Tom strutted right after him.

"Your place is in the henhouse," Red insisted. "Now let me be."

"Every hero needs an assistant," said Big Tom, as if it were a fact like the sun'll come up tomorrow. "Paul Bunyan had Babe the Blue Ox. Pecos Bill had his horse Widowmaker."

Red still wasn't convinced. "What about Davy Crockett?"

"Why, he had his coonskin cap," Big Tom replied.

Well, Red couldn't argue with the truth. He slung his provisions over Tom's wing and hopped on his back, and the two of them went off to seek their fortunes.

They could've picked a better day for it. Hadn't been on the road but an hour and a half before a big raindrop spattered Red's fresh new haircut. Before they knew it, they were awash in a gully by the side of the road.

"Fine way to start our new careers," clucked Tom as they scrambled for higher ground.

"If all you can do is complain," said Red, "then you can just scoot on back to the henhouse. At least Davy Crockett's assistant kept his head dry."

"Oh, all right," Tom sighed, and extended his wing to shelter Red from the driving rain. Red sniffled a little. He was coming down with a cold, which made his usually marvelous nose as useless as his appendix. So it was Tom who first smelled the two soggy but well-dressed city types coming down the road toward them.

"Food, Julius!" said the sturdy-looking woman, thinking of a Tom fricassee. "Our prayers are answered!"

"Don't count your chickens," said Red from behind Tom's wing.

"A talking chicken!" exclaimed her tall companion. "Our fortunes are made, El!"

"Wrong again," said Red.

The woman stooped down and had a look. "Ow!" she screamed when Tom pecked her on the forehead.

"Serves you right," grumped Red, stepping out from his shelter. "What's your business, strangers?"

The two travelers realized their mistake and shook their heads sadly. "Excuse us, man mountain," the woman apologized with a majestic curtsy. "We meant no disrespect. If I had the sense I was born with, I'd've realized chickens can't talk."

"Of course they can," said Red, folding his arms across his chest. "They don't speak the same language as you, is all."

"Exactly what Elsinore meant to say, I'm sure," said the man. "I'm Julius Caesarius Dotterer. This is my sister Elsinore. We're the wettest, weariest travelers in the history of mankind, and our hunger must've afflicted our brains. You wouldn't by any chance have a morsel you could spare, would you?"

"Do you like corn?" Red asked, totally ignoring Tom's suspicious cackling.

"On the cob, off the cob, cream style, chowder, fritters, pone, pudding, or popped," replied Elsinore.

"Likewise," Julius agreed.

Red dug into his sack and handed them each a kernel. "I'm afraid it's all we can spare. We have a long way to go."

Julius and El were touched. They savored the kernels as if they were bonbons. They thanked Red over and over and allowed as how they owed him a favor. "Where might you be going?" asked Elsinore.

"Don't really know," said Red. "Anywhere there's a fortune to be made, I guess."

"A fortune?" said Elsinore. "We know where you can find that, all right."

"Permit me," said Julius, picking Red up and lifting him to eye level. "You see, we're walking to Providence in search of employment. Perhaps you and your friend would care to join us."

Before Red could reply, he sneezed so hard he fell off Julius's palm. Big Tom rushed right over, and Red landed on his feathered back. "Are you all right?" Tom clucked.

"I guess so," said Red.

"Now you know why you need an assistant," Tom scolded.

"Gesundheit," said Julius when he finished wiping his face. He stooped down to Red. "Will you come with us?"

"I'll have to consult my assistant," said Red. And he explained the entire proposition to Tom.

Now, the only word of human that rooster understood was "dinnertime," but he'd already caught the drift of what was going on between Red and the strangers, and he didn't like it much. Red's explanation certainly didn't change his mind any.

"If you didn't have the sniffles," Tom told Red, "you'd smell something funny, too."

"If you understood human," Red shot back, "you'd know there's no harm in 'em. They'd like our company."

"They'd like my neck," Tom protested. "That woman started drooling the moment she laid eyes on me."

[49]

"Do what you please," said Red. "I'm going to Providence."

"Then I'll go, too," said Tom. "But don't say I didn't warn you."

The rain let up. Red rode in style in Julius's lapel pocket. Big Tom did the best he could on top of Elsinore's head, but it was a little too much like being Davy Crockett's assistant for comfort. He suffered in silence as Red recounted the particulars of his life so far, a thing he always had to do for strangers. By the time Red got to the part where he'd left the farm on account of the farmer wouldn't give him that raise— that is, rather, 'cause he had this huge yen to travel— the sun had dried everybody out. Tom was snoring and nearly fell from his perch when Elsinore shrieked, "Providence!"

Anyhow, that's what the sign said, but it looked pretty much like anywhere else to Red. "Doesn't look like much to me," he said, disappointed.

"Patience," said Julius.

They walked on a ways, and sure enough, the houses started getting bigger and fancier, like nothing Red had ever seen. After a while, every house had a big grassy lawn, and curlicued columns, and filigreed iron gates with people in brass buttons to open 'em.

"Well, my lad," said Julius, "here's fortune aplenty. All you need to do is find a way to attach yourself to some of it."

"What do you and your sister do for a living?" Red asked.

"We, sir, are servants," Julius replied, bowing so deeply Red nearly fell out of his pocket. "Elsinore is a cook and, if need be, a chambermaid. I am a butler by profession."

"I guess I know what a cook is," said Red, "but what exactly does a butler do?"

"Why, he buttles, of course!" replied Elsinore indignantly.

"Oh," said Red, ashamed to be so ignorant.

"The butler is the overseer of the servants, Mr.

Red," Julius informed him. "He is the keeper of the keys, and he performs such important functions as the opening of doors."

Now, turning doorknobs and holding a couple of key chains sounded to Red like a pretty soft way to make his fortune, so he asked Julius how you went about getting such a job as that. "There are numerous methods," Julius told him. "Most require long, laborious years of industry and toil in positions of somewhat less responsibility."

Red frowned; it didn't seem so easy after all.

"However," Julius went on, "if one has the talent and the desire, one may rise quickly. Why don't you seek employment with us?"

"I guess we could give it a try," Red said. And they began tramping up and down the streets of Providence to find out who needed a servant or four.

There were plenty of SERVANTS WANTED signs on those iron gates, but the folks who lived behind 'em were mighty particular about who they'd hire. The first ones liked Julius and Elsinore well enough, and they thought they could find something for Tom to do, but they told Red they couldn't possibly use him, since they needed somebody tall enough to change light bulbs without a lot of fuss. Julius and Elsinore carried their friends out in a huff.

At the next mansion, the owners would've been delighted to have Red, since they figured he could give their cockroaches a good talking-to. But they refused to allow Big Tom anywhere on the premises, for fear he might beat up their prize pussycat.

Red and his friends remained unemployed. Down and up the streets of Providence they tramped, but everywhere it was the same story: Red or Tom didn't fit in, one or the other. Sometimes both. "It's awfully hard to find a job when you're hooked up with a midget and a fryer," Elsinore complained, but Julius, always the gent, gave her one of his withering stares and made her apologize. Red felt better for a little while—until Elsinore pointed out a sign that read:

SERVANTS WANTED

CHICKENS AND SHRIMP NEED NOT APPLY

When she finished reading it to him, Red jumped down from Julius's pocket, ripped the sign from the fence, and shredded it into kindling. He was so angry he yanked out one of the iron fence posts and bent it into a pretzel. "Prejudice!" he cried. "Nothing makes me madder!" And he would have stripped the buttons from the gateman's fancy coat if Tom hadn't reminded him how late it was getting.

They'd worn out quite a bit more shoe leather by the time they noticed an elderly little fellow with a white goatee chasing a liveried man and woman out his gate. "Get out, you scallions!" he shouted. "Be-gone, and good rodents!" And he emphasized his point by thrashing his cane in the air.

"I say, what seems to be the trouble?" Julius shouted to the fleeing butler.

"He's loony!" the butler shouted back, and ran down the street.

"He's mad!" screamed the maid, following close on his heels.

"You're darned right I'm mad!" roared the old gent with the whiskers as he stopped to catch his breath. "They forgot the marshmallows on my afternoon tea!"

"Shocking!" said Elsinore.

"Unheard of!" agreed Julius.

"Daffy!" is what Red thought, but he kept it to himself.

"And now I'm without my servants *and* my marshmallows," the little man grumped. "Where could I possibly find any on such short notice?"

"Marshmallows?" Elsinore asked.

"Those, too," said the crotchety old fellow.

Naturally, Julius had the solution to his problems.

But Captain Sanford said he never hired anybody without letting him know what he was in for. "I demand just three things from life," he said firmly. "A bath every Tuesday, clean socks every Wednesday, and a cup of tea with marshmallows every afternoon at four o'clock sharp. Anyone who goofs up on one of those three necessities becomes my mortal enemy from that day forward."

Julius and Elsinore held a little conference and decided they wouldn't have too much trouble meeting those demands.

"Done!" cried Captain Sanford, poking Big Tom with his cane. "Now, what about this cocky rooster of yours?"

"We were coming to that," Julius said hesitantly.

"Let him speak for himself," said the Captain. He stooped down and clucked a few words to Tom in a honey-dipped accent. "So you want to work for me, eh?"

Tom was astonished. "Where'd you learn our language?" he demanded.

"Why, my business was chickens," the Captain explained. "I bought and sold more of your brothers and sisters and aunts and uncles and third cousins once removed than I care to count. Chickens made me wealthy."

Tom frowned. "Somehow, I don't think we'd get along."

"Now, there's where you're wrong. I'm retired nowadays. Sold the chicken business lock, stock, and frying pan. Everything I have, I owe to chickens, so I'm rather kindly disposed towards 'em. In fact, I love chickens, and I don't just mean fried."

Tom was still kind of suspicious. "What sort of job do you have in mind for me?"

"Always needed an exterminator around here, and you could be him. Hunt and peck out those pesky grubs and termites when they bother us."

"Well, I don't know. . . ."

"Don't fret about my former profession any longer. Why, you're the brand of tough old bird we used to reject even for our stockpots. Besides, it's been so long since I last spoke chicken, I've nearly forgotten how. You and I can have a little polite conversation now and again to keep me abreast. What do you say?"

"Red'll have to agree."

"Red? Who's Red?"

"Me," said Red, standing tall in Julius's pocket.

"Who said that?" demanded the Captain, putting on his bifocals.

"I did," said Red.

When the Captain took a look, his bifocals fell off and his moustache stood on end. "Well, I'll be!" he shouted, staring Red right in the eye. "Sonny!"

"I don't believe it!" I exclaimed.

The farmer filled my glass and chuckled. "Neither did Red."

CHAPTER FIVE

RED FINDS HIS FORTUNE

Why, Red looked like somebody'd hit him over the head with a two-by-four. He couldn't think of a single thing to say.

"Well, don't just stand there," boomed the Captain. "Give your pappy a hug!"

"But—but—how could you—" Red stammered.

"Be your daddy?" the Captain interrupted. "Easiest thing in the world to explain!"

But Captain Sanford was so overcome with joy it took him till quarter to sundown to get the whole story out. The gist was that he and Mrs. Sanford were always so busy with their chicken business that they never thought much about having kids, and when they finally did get around to it, they were pretty well up in years and more or less set in their ways. So when Mrs. Sanford finally gave birth to a baby boy, it made for quite a sizable change in their lives.

No sooner had the Captain finished passing out the stogies than his newborn offspring commenced to squall and bawl and keep them up till all hours like a fly you can't swat down. The Captain got used to it pretty quick, seeing as how he'd spent many a sleepless night in henhouses that weren't exactly as peaceful as your average mausoleum. But his Mrs. had what she called "refined sensibilities," and she didn't enjoy having to spend the better part of her day just trying to sneak a little beauty rest.

Now, all this was before the Captain had made his fortune. What he had in the bank back then didn't amount to chicken feed. Naturally, he and the Mrs. couldn't afford a nurse or a nanny to take care of their boy, and they had to do all the feeding and diapering and burping themselves. They got pretty darned sick of it, too, especially Mrs. Sanford. As she put it after a week or so, "At least you don't have to diaper chickens."

Well, since this was the first baby the Captain and his Mrs. ever had, and since most of the young'uns they'd known up till then were hatchling chicks, they figured their boy was more or less normal for a newborn. And for a while nobody thought to tell 'em any different. But the very first time Mrs. Sanford took her baby out for a stroll in his carriage, a nosy passerby took one look inside and said to her, "That's the tiniest baby I've ever seen. Why, he must be a freak of nature."

Now, Mrs. Sanford had a temper like a hungry gorilla, and she wasn't about to stand idly by and see her son insulted. She let go of the carriage for a second and socked that fellow right in the nose. By the time the two of 'em stopped arguing, the carriage was rolling right down Neutacankanut Hill. Mrs. Sanford chased after it, but it kept rolling faster and faster, and finally it rolled right over the cliff into the Woonasquatucket River.

Needless to say, that was the last the Sanfords ever saw of their son. The Captain and his wife were pretty broke up about it for a while, and they gave some thought to having another baby, but the Mrs. finally decided that since at first they didn't succeed, there wasn't much point in trying again, and besides, she was darned if she'd ever change a diaper again as long as she lived. Since the Captain thought it'd be pretty hard for him to have a baby all by himself, he didn't think much about it after that. The Sanfords devoted themselves wholeheartedly to their chickens, and the only day the Captain ever regretted it was the day Mrs. Sanford choked to death on a wishbone.

"And that's the whole story," said the Captain as the sun dipped below the horizon.

"But then, how did I get to the Huckabys' hen-house?" Red wanted to know.

"The where? The who? Search me!" the Captain answered. "You always were a tough'un. Maybe you crawled!"

Maybe he did at that. Anyhow, Red guessed that was as good an explanation as anybody could come up with without invoking strange and mysterious powers, so he let it be.

"Are we hired?" he asked.

"Hired? Well, your friends are, of course. But you won't have to do another lick of work in your lifetime. You're rich, son. Rich!"

Red knew a good deal when he heard it. He reached out, put his arms around his pappy's nose, and hugged it so hard the Captain lost his sense of smell for the better part of an hour. When Red's dad finally got his breath back, he thanked Julius and Elsinore for being so loyal to his son, and he promised them lifetime positions—provided they never omitted his three necessities. He thanked Tom profusely in chicken, and he was delighted beyond all telling when Tom let him know that Red could cackle with the best of 'em. The three chicken-talkers had a glorious time exchanging some of the riddles fowl find funny, such as "Why did the farmer cross the road?" and "Why don't chickens wear red suspenders?" and so on.

Well, it was getting late, and there wasn't time for Elsinore to fix dinner, so the Captain took everyone out to the finest restaurant in Providence. At first the headwaiter refused to seat the little gentleman in coveralls, but the Captain made such a fuss that they let Red in even though he wasn't wearing a jacket and tie. Of course, Tom didn't have any problem that way. His close-fitting feathered coat and blue satin neckpiece were the height of fashion.

Well, that restaurant pretty near bowled Red over. Between the blazing chandeliers and the waiters in penguin suits and the fancy silk brocade on the walls, he didn't know where to look first. And when he sat down on top of a dozen Paris phone books and the waiter handed him a menu about six times taller than he was, Red almost wished he'd taken those etiquette lessons from Professor Wigglesworth.

"What's for supper?" Red asked his newfound father.

"You can have anything on the menu," said the Captain.

Red saw a lot of ink on his menu, but it didn't look too appetizing. He did find a tasty little spot of gravy and lapped it up. But even though it was delicious, Red had to admit he was still hungry.

"Perfectly understandable," said the Captain. "Let's ask our waiter what's tonight's specialty."

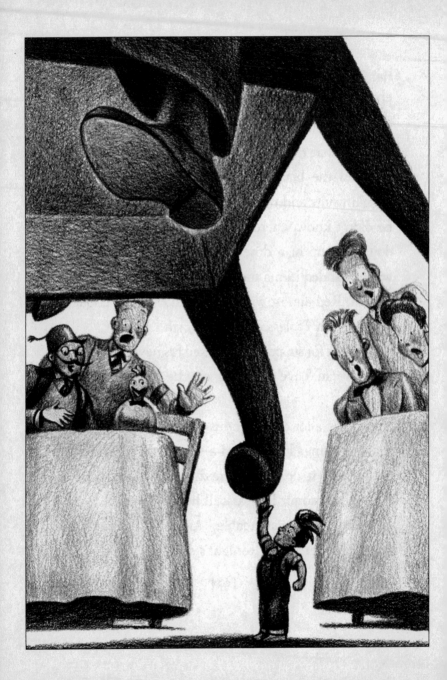

"*Coq au vin*, monsieur," the waiter replied.

"Huh?" said Red.

"A young, tender chicken—"

"Not in mixed company," Red interrupted. "Make mine lobster, thanks."

"Very good, monsieur. And for *le roostair? Du popcorn*, perhaps?"

The Captain translated for Big Tom, and Tom reckoned popcorn would be fine and dandy with him.

Well, when the appetizer came, Red thought he heard some wisenheimer at another table say, "Look at that shrimp eating that shrimp cocktail." When Red started in on his soup, he was almost positive he heard that same smart aleck declare, "Now I know who put his overalls in Mrs. Murphy's chowder." Red pretended not to hear, but when his Maine course arrived, he caught the nincompoop saying, "He's lucky that lobster doesn't swallow *him*."

Red turned redder than his dinner. He jumped down to the floor, strode across to the next table, grabbed

[67]

the leg of that wise guy's chair, and yanked with all his might. The chair collapsed, and the big jerk crashed to the floor. Best of all, that loudmouth's wig went flying and made a splash landing in his neighbor's vichyssoise. Everyone in the restaurant applauded, and Red took a little bow.

The Captain beamed proudly. "Takes after his late mother," he said.

His son returned to finish his dinner in peace.

CHAPTER SIX

RED'S FIRST LOVE

Now, Red never'd given much thought to what it'd be like to be rich. Figured it'd be pretty much the same as being poor, only more so. So when he got back to the Captain's mansion and went inside, he had no idea what to expect.

For a minute he thought he'd walked into a fairy tale. Hundreds of crystal eggs dangled from chandeliers even fancier than the ones he'd seen at the restaurant. The brass door knocker was shaped like a rooster's comb. The doorknobs looked like hens' feet. And the silver faucet handles were modeled after baby chicks.

There were portraits of famous fowls of history on

every wall. They were so lifelike Big Tom immediately fell in love with the eight-foot-tall blue hen in the dining room. And Red was so amazed to find hot water coming out of the bathroom faucets that he took two baths that night, one right after the other, even though the Captain insisted that a good scrubdown every Tuesday was more than enough for anybody.

Next morning, Red's eyes popped out a little farther when the Captain gave him a tour of the five-hole golf course in the backyard. "I could afford the other thirteen," the Captain explained, "but they won't all fit in this great state of ours, so I just kind of let 'em slide."

It turned out being rich took a lot of getting used to. Tailors came in and made fancy suits to Red's measure, but he never liked any of 'em half so well as his blue denim britches. Elsinore cooked up dishes he could hardly pronounce, but Red would've been just as happy scrabbling for corn with a flock of hungry chickens. Julius bathed him and combed his hair and sprayed him with something that smelled like roses, but Red would just as soon've washed in a pig trough and slicked his hair down with a little axle grease and smelled like a cross between a human and a chicken and a hog and a wagon wheel the way he used to. And fond as he was of his dad, Red often thought he'd start squawking like a loon if he had to hear just one more story of how the Captain had made his fortune in the poultry trade.

The main trouble with being rich was that there wasn't much to do with yourself except be proud of all the money you had and think up new ways to spend it. Every now and then the Captain would go out and buy a new car or a new boat or a new dinner table, but the trouble was he already had so many of them he had to build a new garage or a new boathouse or a new dining room to put them in. By now he had seventeen cars and sixteen garages (with one abuilding), thirteen boats and eleven boathouses (with two abuilding), seven dinner tables and three dining

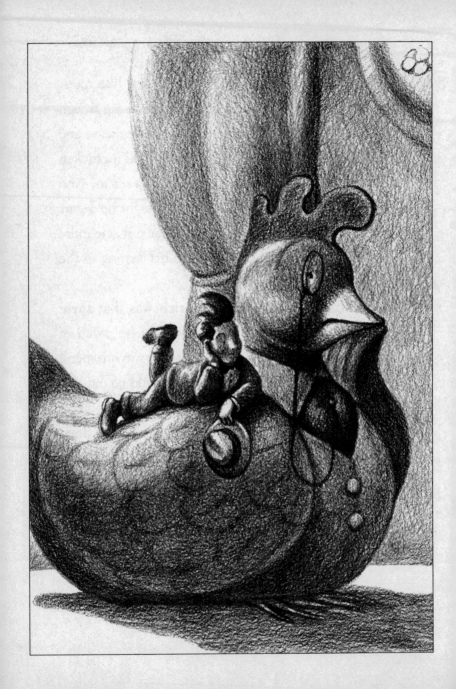

rooms (with one abuilding). He kept the extra dinner tables in the poolroom, the poker room, and the Ping-Pong room.

Red figured he was disappointing his dad because he never could think of anything to spend money on. He had plenty of clothes, he had too much to eat, and he had a roof over his head, which he wasn't all that particular about anyway. He couldn't even buy new cars for his toy train, since it was already so long he had to drive it slow just to keep the engine from ramming the caboose. The only thing Red really had a hankering for was the crescent moon, but when he found somebody who was willing to sell it to him, the Captain stepped in and killed the deal. Red figured he just wasn't cut out to be a spender.

Big Tom didn't mind all the luxury for a while, but when he finally realized his crush on the painting in the dining room was totally useless, he turned bitter. "Fine life this is for a hero!" he would hoot at Red. "Here you stand, dressed up in a monkey suit and smelling like a geranium, while the real heroes are out there fighting the elements and seeking their fortunes."

"But I've found my fortune," Red would reply. "Now what am I supposed to do?"

Tom didn't know the answer, and since he didn't have anything else to do, he'd stalk off to the kitchen and grab a snack. Red usually joined him. By the end of their first month of being rich, they both would've bust their britches if their tailors hadn't come around every week to make 'em new ones.

In fact, Red might've eaten himself into early retirement if it hadn't been for Julius's oversight one Wednesday morning. The butler was so busy remembering the Captain's clean socks he forgot to spritz Red down with that flowery perfume stuff. Well, it was as if somebody'd given Red back his nose.

He took a deep breath and sniffed some beans baking up Boston way. He breathed deeper, and he caught a whiff of a honey tree in Maine up near the Canadian border. Then he inhaled just the slightest little bit, and he smelled the prettiest scent he'd ever run across. Didn't know what it was at first, so he just followed his nose and ended up at the mansion across the street.

He passed the sign that read C. TERWILLIGER, MAYOR, and went up the long walk. There before him on the porch was the loveliest young thing he'd seen or smelled in his entire life.

"Hello, small fry," the damsel greeted him. "Who might you be?"

Red doffed his hat and bowed the way Julius had taught him. "Rhode Island Red, at your service."

Miss Posy Terwilliger flashed the brightest smile and the bluest eyes and the pinkest lips Red had ever seen. He was smitten and smitten but good.

"Will you marry me?" he blurted out.

"You'll have to see my father about that," said the vision of loveliness, and told Red to wait right there while she went inside. A minute or two later, her potbellied father came out.

[75]

"What can I do for you, little fellow?" he asked, pumping Red's arm up and down.

"You can give me your daughter's hand," Red replied.

"I'd gladly throw the rest of her into the bargain, too," said Mayor Terwilliger. "But no man may marry my mademoiselle unless he can pass my test."

"Name it and I will," said Red.

"Not a man before you's managed to succeed, and many's the man that's failed. But if you're still willing to have a go at it, then good luck to you!"

"I'm listening," Red replied.

"I like a man with spunk!" the Mayor exclaimed. "Now, here's the situation. Just four years ago I got elected for the umpty-third time, but now I've got to get elected all over again. It's no picnic, I'll tell you that for certain. Ever kiss a drooling baby? I don't suppose you have. Well, it's no fun at all. And those promises I have to make! Last time, I couldn't think of anything else I hadn't promised yet, so I promised the citizens two chickens in every pot. Now that I'm elected, you'd think they'd be nice and forget all about it, the way they did all my other promises. But no! They expect me to make good on it. People come up to me on the street and say, 'Terwilliger, where's those chickens you promised me?' So that, to make it short, as I'll wager you prefer, is your test."

"What?"

"You put two chickens in every pot in Providence, and my daughter is yours." They shook hands on it.

Well, Red went home and thought it over, and the more he thought, the more he worried. He didn't much care to see his friends and distant relations stewing all over town just because he wanted to marry Terwilliger's lovely daughter. Didn't seem fair to him. So he was on the verge of giving up the whole idea when the wind blew in and he caught a maddening whiff of perfume. He walked back across the street, up Terwilliger's lawn, and onto the porch rail.

"Back so soon?" asked Miss Terwilliger. She sure was pretty.

"Just wanted to make sure you're worth all the fuss," said Red.

"And am I?" She twirled her parasol so fetchingly Red thought he'd crumble right there on the spot.

" 'Fraid so," he said, and went home wondering what he could possibly do. He just had to have that beautiful Terwilliger girl for his wife, but he couldn't betray all of chickendom to do it. He explained to the Captain just what a pickle he was in.

"Easiest thing in the world, son," the Captain boomed. "I'll just buy up every pot in Providence, and then I'll buy enough chickens to fill 'em twice over. And then we'll let 'em all loose."

"I appreciate your offer, Dad," Red said ruefully, "but then *you'd* be the one who could marry Miss Terwilliger. I'm afraid I'll have to pass this test on my own."

"Whatever you think's best," said the Captain. "If I can help, just holler."

Well, Red moped around awhile, and then all of a sudden his eyes lit up like fireflies' behinds. First he told Big Tom the plan, and the rooster thought it was a honey. Then he wired the Huckabys and asked them to put Old Rhody on the next train to Providence.

When that train pulled into the station, Red's entire new family—Tom, the Captain, Elsinore, and Julius— was there to meet it. You should've seen how Rhody carried on. Cried extra-large double-A tears of joy when she saw her little Red again, she did. Couldn't believe he'd done so well for himself in so short a time, but there he was, gussied up like a gentleman, with a whole mob of friends and kinfolk.

The Captain praised Rhody so highly for the care she gave his boy that the hen thought she'd bust from pride. Tom told her he'd never in his life seen such a gorgeous chicken, and he flattered her so unmercifully she turned redder than a fire engine. And though they couldn't speak chicken, Julius and Elsinore were so kind to her she thought maybe she'd died and gone to heaven. Rhody was so pleased she laid two dozen Easter eggs even though it was almost Labor Day.

Next morning, everybody got up early and listened to Red explain his plan. He and Tom and Rhody put on their overalls, and Julius drove them down to the Providence waterfront. Tom and Rhody waited on the doorstep while Red pounded on the first door they came to.

The woman who opened it was so big she could've ended Red's plan just by sitting on 'em, but lucky for him, she didn't. Still, she was mighty surprised to find such short strangers standing on her stoop. "Isn't it a little early for Halloween?" she wondered.

Red couldn't afford to let his temper get the best of him. "No tricks and no treats, ma'am," he said, tipping his cap politely. "I'm the city pot inspector, and these are my assistants. We're here to inspect your pots."

"Well, come right in," said the woman, waddling toward the kitchen. "They're all in here. What're you inspecting 'em for?"

"Oh, cracks, dents, holes—the usual. Then my assistants'll check whether these pots of yours'll be safe for those chickens the Mayor promised you."

"Ha!" she snorted. "I'll see those chickens the day I lay eggs!"

As she handed down her pots, Tom and Rhody stepped into each one, and Red checked it off on a tally sheet. "Do you inspect pans, too?" the woman asked, reaching for a heavy iron skillet on the topmost shelf.

"No, ma'am, we're only authorized for pots," said Red, moving off to one side in case she should happen to slip. "The city pan inspector should be along any day now."

Rhody and Tom finished hopping in and out of all the kitchen pots. "Are there any other pots around here?" Red asked.

"Not a one, unless you count the flowerpots."

"Better do those, too, just to be on the safe side." And Tom and Rhody went to work on 'em while the woman brewed herself and Red a pot of coffee.

"I need your signature," said Red when they were finished. "This certifies that we checked all your pots." He handed her a printed form.

"What's that chicken scratch down there?" she asked.

"Where?"

She pointed. "That tiny little print."

"Looks huge to me."

"Well, I'd imagine. All right, where do I sign?" Red showed her, and she did, and he and the chickens went about their business.

Well, needless to say, it was no easy task. There were quite a few pots in the city of Providence, and one way or another, Tom and Rhody had to squeeze into every last one. They learned not to do their inspecting around mealtimes, 'cause they didn't much enjoy the prospect of wading into steaming caldrons of chicken noodle soup. They learned to be careful not to dip more than their toenails into the smaller vessels after they took the better part of an afternoon getting themselves unstuck from a little girl's dollhouse teapot. They went to houses, restaurants, schools, shops, hardware stores—wherever there was a pot, sooner or later there were Red and Tom and Rhody. They tramped through the city in heat and gloom and mire and got tired and crabby and footsore, but the chickens stuck by Red, and he was grateful to 'em for it.

It took 'em nearly two weeks, which in Rhode Island amounts to a considerable span of time, but they finally finished the task. They went to the Terwilliger mansion first thing next morning. The Mayor's beautiful daughter waved to them as they approached the porch.

"Wash out your wedding dress, angel," Red greeted her. "I've passed the test!"

"Prove it!" stormed her father as he burst out the front door. He didn't believe it for a minute.

Red pointed to the limousine coming up the drive. Julius and Elsinore parked it and unloaded carton after carton of certificates proving once and for all (though in the finest of fine print) that two chickens had at one time or another been in every last pot in Providence.

Terwilliger was shocked. "They haven't been in *my* pots!" he snorted.

But Tom and Rhody were too fast for him. They flew into the kitchen before he could grab 'em, and they began romping through the cupboards.

Well, it was something. Only other time Providence ever saw such a commotion was the Great Hurricane of '38, and that was a gentle zephyr by comparison. Feathers flew, and talons clawed, and pots clanged, and Terwilliger huffed, and Red rassled him, and— hardest of all to believe, but truer than the wind— Julius wrinkled his shirtfront. Anyway, from beanpot to crockpot to cachepot to chamberpot, Tom and Rhody got into 'em all, and Elsinore checked 'em off. Still, Terwilliger wouldn't admit Red'd passed his test till he realized the little fellow was about a sixteenth of an inch away from twisting his nose clean off.

"When's the wedding?" Red demanded.

"There'll be no wedding yet!" Terwilliger declared after he made sure his nose was still on him. "Oh, I admit you passed Part One of my test fair and square. But there's still Part Two to go."

"Part two?" I shouted.

The farmer nodded.

CHAPTER SIX, PART TWO

RED AND THE ELECTION ROOT

"Part Two?" Red shouted. He'd never heard of anything so ridiculous in his entire life.

"I never heard of anything so ridiculous in my entire life," was how he put it to Terwilliger. "You said if I passed your test, your daughter would be mine. And I passed your test."

"Part One," the Mayor reminded him.

"You never said anything about a second part," Red protested.

"You never asked."

Well, he had Red there. The poor little fellow didn't know what to say. He explained the situation to the chickens.

"After all our work!" Rhody huffed indignantly. "It's not fair!"

"Claw his eyes out!" Tom shrieked.

"I've half a mind to do just that, but I doubt it'd help much," Red replied. "Guess I'm just gonna have to pass Part Two." And he asked Terwilliger what he'd have to do to do it.

"Glad to see you're still interested," said the Mayor. "As I've said many times on many different occasions, if there's one thing I like to see in a man, it's spunk."

The Mayor took a deep breath and went on. "Now, the election up ahead looks like a real humdinger. People keep telling me now that the city pot inspector's checked 'em out, they're expecting to get their chickens any day now, and if they don't get 'em by election time, they're gonna hold me personally responsible. So—"

"I've already put two chickens in every one of their pots," Red interrupted, "and I'm not about to do it again."

"And neither am I," said Terwilliger. "No, it looks as though there's only one way I'm likely to win this election. And that's to get myself a good fresh supply of election root."

"What's election root?" Red asked.

Terwilliger took the "Egg–Fowl" volume of the encyclopedia down from its shelf. "Elbow grease . . . elderberry . . . El Dorado . . . here we are!" And he read from the book:

ELECTION ROOT: *Dogcatchium supernumerarius*

A mildly toxic weed of the jimson family, found near cranberry bogs and believed to possess certain supernatural properties. The candidate for a given office who ingests the largest quantity of election root during a campaign is said to be unbeatable at the polls.

Since this plant offers the only known symptomatic relief of the disease known as election fever, the great demand for it among politicians has rendered it virtually extinct. Its Latin name derives from a surprising Rhode Island election in which an unsavory character by the name of "Stinky Sam" Stanky, who most observers claimed "could not be elected dogcatcher," in fact won the position by an overwhelming majority. For years thereafter, Mr. Stanky claimed he owed his victory to his prodigious consumption of election root, although many observers believed that the fact that he ran unopposed may have been a more important factor.

See also: Dogcatchers, Famous; Roots, Magical; Weeds, Useful.

Terwilliger slammed the book shut.

"I know heroes aren't supposed to say this," said Red, "but I don't get it."

"Simple. All you need to do to pass Part Two of my test is find me enough election root to get me re-elected."

"And then I'll get your daughter's hand?"

"Naturally."

"No tricks?" Red asked suspiciously.

"Who, me?" replied the Mayor.

" 'Scuse me a minute." Red went to the front doorway and gazed out at the lovely Miss Terwilliger.

"It's not polite to stare," she told him, arching her lovely eyebrows.

"Didn't mean to be rude. I'm trying to figure whether it's worth going through another long ordeal just to make you my bride."

"And?" she asked, exposing a tiny sliver of the whitest teeth Red'd ever laid eyes on.

" 'Fraid so, darn it."

Red went back inside. "Guess I'll go for it," he told the Mayor.

"Spunky as ever," said Terwilliger.

Elsinore belched mildly to get Red's attention. "Pardon me, Mr. Red, but I think you ought to ask the gentleman whether he's gonna double-cross you again."

"That is to say," Julius broke in, "are there any additional parts or terms or conditions to this test of his?"

"Nope," said Terwilliger. "Part One and Part Two. That's the whole shebang." He and Red shook on it.

"Do you have any idea where I might find some of this election root?" Red asked him.

"Why, this is a test, now. Wouldn't be fair for me to give you any hints. But good luck to you!" And Terwilliger escorted them all out the door.

Now, it happened that the Captain had been quite

a gardener. In his day, he'd been famous throughout Rhode Island for his prize-winning eggplant. So he knew what kind of picklement Red was in.

"You won't find any election root around here, I'm sorry to say," he told his son. "Nobody's seen any for nigh unto forty years. It's extinct. Done for. All gone."

"*Virtually* extinct, sir, if the encyclopedia is not in error," Julius corrected him.

"Well, if there's a lick of election root in the entire state of Rhode Island, I'll be kerblozzled," Captain Sanford declared.

Elsinore brought in the evening paper and read the screaming headline. " 'TERWILLIGER'S DEFEAT LIKELY,' " she announced. " 'Opponent Buzwinkle Takes Wide Lead in Poll.' "

"Maybe Buzwinkle's been eating election root," Red suggested.

"All he has to eat is two square meals a day to whip a houndrel like that Terwilliger," said the Captain.

"I'm voting for Buzwinkle, and I don't know a soul who's doing otherwise. You'll have to find your man a carload of election root if you expect to get him elected."

Red didn't know what to do. Election day was getting closer by the minute, and he didn't have the foggiest idea how he'd catch him any *Dogcatchium.* Finally he decided he'd get himself some wading boots and just take his chances in the cranberry bogs. Rhody didn't want him to, since she was afraid he'd catch cold, and Tom didn't want him to, since as Red's assistant he was obliged to go along, and though he still had his taste for adventure, he preferred to find it where it was warm and dry. But Red's mind was like one of those night locks they have in the bank: Once he got it set, there was nothing anybody could do to change it. So Red and Tom had hip boots made to measure, and off they went to the cranberry bogs.

Up and down the bogs they tramped, living on a diet of corn and cranberries, but not a sprig of election root did they see. The local chickens had never heard of it, since the head man among 'em generally made his way to the top by fighting and didn't care about popularity one way or the other. Red thought maybe somebody could tell him what election root smelled like, so he could sniff it out with his nose, but only a few of the people they asked had even heard tell of the stuff. A few old-timers tried to help, but the last time they'd seen election root was so long ago they could hardly remember what it looked like. One man said it smelled like huckleberry ice cream, and another thought it had the aroma of roast duck, and an old woman was positive the odor was a cross between gumballs and pickled herring. Red finally just gave up on the idea that his nose would be any use to him at all this time.

So Red and Tom just used their eyes and their feet as they slogged among the cranberries, looking for a plant that seemed to have gone the way of the dodo. Election day kept getting nearer and nearer, and autumn was rushing in wet and nippy, and Red was so frustrated he was beginning to think he'd never get to the root of his problem. He and Tom were grumbling at each other when they ran across an old farmer baling cranberries.

"Let me give you a hand with that," Red offered.

"Much obliged, stranger. Where you headed?"

"Nowhere in particular. I'm looking for some election root."

"Election root! Save your feet! You'll not find any of that in the state of Rhode Island, or anywhere else this side of Jupiter. Believe me, I know. Used to be commissioner of this county, and the year I ran out of election root, the citizens dropped me like a bad habit—which I guess I was, come to think of it. I've been looking to get some of that stuff these last twenty years, and I can tell you, there's just none to be found."

"Isn't there any anywhere? I'm desperate."

"What're *you* running for?"

"The hand of the Mayor's daughter."

"Terwilliger, eh! So that's how it is!"

Red nodded bravely.

"Well, tell you what you do," the farmer said. "Forget all about election root. Just go find yourself a whole mess of jack-in-the-pulpit—you know, the one that looks like a politician right up there on the old soapbox—and give your man as many of the leaves as he can swallow. Tell him it's election root. He won't know the difference."

"But does it work?"

"Been known to. It's not a hundred percent effective, mind you, but it just might do the trick. Besides, maybe your man'll get elected anyhow."

"Not much chance of that," said Red.

"It's as bad as that, is it? Well, as the voice of hard experience, let me tell you, friend, you never know. And if he does figure out a way to win, you may as well let on as if the stuff you gave him had something to do with it. Which, as I say, it's been known to. Just be sure he eats plenty of it first thing every morning, and second thing all day long, and whatever you do, don't let his opponent get ahold of any. And stay away from it yourself or you'll wish you had."

Well, it wasn't exactly what Red wanted to hear, but it sounded something like good sense to him, so he and Tom stripped the leaves off a whole field of jack-in-the-pulpit and phoned Julius to bring a car and pick them up.

When he got there, Julius read them the grim news in the latest edition of the Providence paper. " 'BUZWINKLE HOLDS ASTOUNDING LEAD. Terwilliger Desperate; Promises Chicken Delivery Day After Election.' "

"Well, maybe this stuff'll work some magic," Red sighed.

"Is it really election root?" Julius asked.

"Close enough," Red replied.

When they drove back through town, the first thing they noticed was a rally for Oliver T. Buzwinkle, Man of the People, but they didn't stop to listen to what he had to say. It didn't matter anyhow; since so many people were whooping and cheering and applauding, you couldn't hear the candidate above the crowd.

Two blocks down the street, Mayor Terwilliger, Man of the Chickens, was holding a rally of his own. You could hear him just fine, since the only people nearby were three sleepy reporters and his beautiful daughter. "I promise the people of this fair city that if I am elected their mayor for another four-year term," Terwilliger bombasted, "I will personally see to it that they will have not only two chickens in every pot, but a turkey in every oven as well."

"How do you plan to accomplish this, Mr. Mayor?" asked one reporter wearily.

"By keeping a tight rein on the fiscal budget!" Terwilliger boomed.

Red got out of the limousine and mooned at Miss Terwilliger till her father was through with his speech.

Then he led the Mayor to the car and opened the trunk.

"You don't mean . . ." exclaimed Terwilliger.

"I do indeed," Red said.

"Doesn't look quite the way I remembered it," Terwilliger noted.

"It's a slightly different variety," Red hedged. Of course, the last thing a genuine hero would do is lie. Might semifib now and again, though, while keeping his fingers crossed.

"Well," said Terwilliger, scratching his head, "the way things are going, if I eat that stuff and I manage to win, there's no question about it. That'd have to be election root, all right."

"We'll unload it up at your house," said Red. "Eat as much as you like as often as you like, but be sure to have at least ten big leaves first thing every morning."

"Lad, I'll be at that stuff every waking minute,"

Terwilliger replied. "I don't know what I could do to repay you if I win."

"Oh, yes, you do," Red reminded him.

Well, the first thing the Mayor did when he got home was have an election root salad. He followed it with some election root soup, a big helping of election root casserole, a good-sized bowl of election root pudding, and half an election root pie à la mode. It all tasted rotten, really bitter compared with the election root he remembered from way back, but he reminded himself that maybe his memory wasn't as good as it used to be.

"More!" he hollered to the cook, but nobody answered him.

"I say, bring me more election root!" he yelled, but that didn't bring results, either.

"Cook!" he screamed at the top of his lungs, and then all of a sudden he realized what'd happened. His mouth had swollen up, and he couldn't say a word.

When he screamed, all that came out was a little squeak like when you squeeze a rubber duck. Talking in a normal tone didn't work, either. And when he whispered, it just sounded like wind whistling through the leaves. He sent for the doctor.

"Mayor Terwilliger," said the medic after he'd peered down the politician's throat, "my opinion is that you've lost your voice. Would you like to pay me now, or should I send you a bill?"

"What can you do to get my voice back?" Terwilliger scribbled on a notepad.

"I can tell you to shut up for a few days. You've probably been giving too many speeches."

"But I'm a politician! Isn't there anything you can do?" Terwilliger wrote.

"I can bill you seventy-five dollars for this house call. Good day, Mr. Mayor," said the doctor, and he went out the door. Mayor Terwilliger was so angry he wolfed down six platefuls of election root stew.

Now, Buzwinkle kept hearing everybody tell him

how sure it was he'd beat Terwilliger, and it wasn't long before he began to get cocky. He called Mayor Terwilliger "an old bag of tricks," "a chicken-livered ninny," "a turkey neck," and a few other things even the newspapers wouldn't print. But when the reporters went around to see what the Mayor had to say about all that, his daughter told them in a melodious voice Red could hear from across the street that her father had no comment.

"But he always has a comment," one reporter protested.

"Not today," said Miss Posy Terwilliger, so fetchingly that Red nearly fainted.

"I guess there's a first time for everything," sniffed the reporter. "Most unusual, though."

Well, when he heard Terwilliger was clamming up, Buzwinkle just knew he had him licked. He told the crowd he wanted them to know exactly what to expect from the forthcoming Buzwinkle administration. So he promised them not only two chickens in every pot and a turkey in every oven, but also a steak on every barbecue. A reporter asked him how he'd possibly be able to do all this. "By keeping a tight rein on the fiscal budget," Buzwinkle replied.

Though Mayor Terwilliger was dying to tell everyone he'd give them everything Buzwinkle had promised plus two dozen oysters in every stew, he still hadn't found his voice, so he had to issue another "no comment." Some of the townspeople began to wonder if Buzwinkle wasn't promising a little too much.

Next morning, the Mayor polished off an enormous bowl of cornflakes and election root, and his voice wasn't the least bit better. Downtown, Buzwinkle mounted his platform and announced that his administration would pave every sidewalk in Providence with gold the moment he was elected. If only his voice'd been working, Terwilliger would've promised gold pavement on the sidewalks *and* the streets, but once again, the Mayor didn't have any comment about his opponent's remarks. People got the feeling maybe Buzwinkle was guaranteeing more than he could deliver.

Red dropped in on Mayor Terwilliger every day to make sure he was eating his election root and to sneak a peek at Miss Posy. Every day, the newspapers came out with headlines like TERWILLIGER NARROWS GAP and BUZWINKLE LEAD EVAPORATES and MAYORALTY CONTEST NECK AND NECK. Terwilliger half suspected it was the election root that was making him so hoarse, but the stuff was working so well otherwise, he didn't dare stop eating it.

In the last week of the campaign, Buzwinkle's disappearing lead so frightened him that he promised two cars in every garage, two garages in every home, two homes in every family, and two chocolate bars in every lunchbox. Terwilliger longed to go him one better by promising two years of vacation for every worker, but his voice was worse than ever, and he couldn't comment at all. Red heard people say that whatever else was wrong with Terwilliger, at least he didn't seem to be off his rocker. So maybe, just maybe, the election root would work and he would pass Part Two.

On the last day of the campaign, a high wind howled through the streets of Providence, but Red and a few other hardy souls risked getting blown away just to see what the challenger would promise today. "My friends and supporters," Buzwinkle shouted above the wind, "you have all heard my campaign platform, and you can be certain every one of my promises will be carried out the moment I am elected. But in the heat of the campaign, I forgot my most important pledge to you, the voters of this fair city. I pledge to you, here and now, that during my term of office, it will never snow in the city of Providence."

Almost on cue, a few whitish flakes fluttered down from above. "Let's see you stop it!" shouted someone in the group. You certainly wouldn't call it a crowd.

"I can't, without the power of the Mayor's office! I'm not elected yet!" Buzwinkle cried.

[105]

"And you won't be, you fool, if we have anything to say about it!" another heckler hollered back. The wind kicked up again, and the snow turned to sleet, and the few hardy souls began to look for cover.

"No rain, either!" Buzwinkle shouted desperately. "Blue skies every day!" But only Red was left to hear him.

Well, it snowed and snowed till it was all anybody could do just to get out the front door on election day, but most of the citizens of Providence found some way or other to get themselves down to the polls. Even though he was a year or two shy of voting age, Red went down there with the Captain, and Tom went, too, even though chickens didn't have the franchise. As they were leaving, Mayor Terwilliger came in to cast his ballot. People shook his hand and thanked him for conducting such a gentlemanly campaign, and he shook theirs back and nodded his head and smiled, but right to the last, he didn't say a word.

You could look it up in the library. "TERWILLIGER WINS BY AVALANCHE." "BIGGEST POLITICAL COMEBACK IN RHODE ISLAND HISTORY." "BUZWINKLE CLAIMS ELECTION FRAUD." The papers all said it was on account of the Mayor's brilliant strategy of giving Buzwinkle enough rope to hang himself. But Terwilliger and Red knew full well he owed his victory to the peculiar properties of his personal variety of election root.

The day after the election, Red dropped by the Terwilliger mansion to claim his prize. Miss Terwilliger was shivering a little in her customary place on the porch, but somehow her rosy cheeks and fuzzy earmuffs and big fur coat made her look more lovely than ever. "Pack your trousseau, sweetie pie," Red greeted her jauntily.

Her father came out the door before she had a chance to reply. His voice was still a little froggy, but it was a whole lot better than it'd been. "Red," said the Mayor, beaming, "I want to shake your hand. I don't know how or where you found it, but that election root saved me my job."

"Guess I passed Part Two, all right."

"With flying colors, my boy."

"Well, you know what I'm here for."

"Yes," said the Mayor, "and I don't know how to break the news."

"Huh?"

"Well, it's . . . I mean . . . to sum up . . . Oh, fact is, she won't have you."

"But you said—"

"I know, and I'm sick about it. But she's got her mind made up that if she ever walks down that aisle, it'll be with a big, tall, handsome type. Don't ask me why. I told her you beat such fellows seven ways from Sunday, but she just won't listen."

"I'll bet I could convince her."

"Bet you could if anybody could, but you'd yell yourself hoarse before you turned the trick. When she saw you coming up the walk, she stuffed cotton in her ears, and she glued those earmuffs on. Right now, she's as deaf as your hat."

Red was so confused he nearly cried. "But . . . but you promised!"

"My heavens! If there's one thing I thought you'd learned by now, it's not to put much stock in a politician's promise."

What could Red say to that? He could've beaten the Mayor up, but he didn't really want to go to jail, and it wouldn't've been very herolike anyhow. When he glanced over toward Miss Posy Terwilliger, his little heart made a sound like a twig snapping. He hung his head so low his chin scraped the ground, and he trudged back across the street. "Pack your bags," he told Tom. "We're going back to the country."

"Just when I was getting comfortable around here," Tom complained. He leaned back on the couch and popped a grape into his craw, but he could see how downhearted Red looked and knew it was no use arguing.

"Stick around!" the Captain insisted when he'd found out what happened. "There's plenty more clams in the sea!"

"Don't go!" cried Elsinore. "Who'll remind me to put the marshmallows in Captain Sanford's tea?"

"Please reconsider," Julius urged. "Whom will I hunt Easter eggs with?"

"You belong here, the way I belong in the Huckabys' henhouse," Rhody cackled. "Doesn't seem right to up and leave just because you've had a little disappointment."

But Red's mind was set. "Oh, I know I seem like an ingrate and a bad egg, but I'm not, really. I'll never forget all you folks've done for me, and I know I'll be back again. But right now the city's a little too much for me, and I need to get back to the country and think things out in peace." He and Tom pecked every-

body good-bye, and then they loped down the path.

Well, they walked and walked, but Tom could see that Red didn't feel much like talking, so he let him be. When they got to the outskirts of town, Red mumbled, "Guess I'll live."

"You know," Tom remarked, "I didn't want to say anything before. But with that powerful nose of yours, how come you didn't smell out those darned Terwilligers from the very first?"

"I guess a little perfume can hide a whole lot of stink." Red laughed, and Tom knew everything was going to be all right.

A lot of folks say Red really grew up after that. Not on the outside, mind you. He never grew a bit that way. But all the same, he grew up. Of course, he still had his faults, same as anybody else, but from then on his career as a hero really began in earnest. It was right about then that all his really famous adventures started happening.

"Well, go on!" I shouted. "Tell me about the time Red met up with Paul Bunyan."

All of a sudden the rain let up, and the full moon shone through the window like the high beam of a headlight. "Hadn't you best be getting along?" the farmer asked me. "I'm tuckered out, myself."

"But I want to hear about the time Red whipped Paul and John Henry and Pecos Bill all at once."

"I'm pretty dry from all this talking."

"Have some rainwater, then."

"Wouldn't you know it? I'm fresh out," he said, turning the bottle upside down to prove it. "Besides, you've used up the margins of all those old papers, and I'm out of them, too. Why don't you come back another time?"

"I'll write on the walls!" I cried. "I want to spread Red's story far and wide. He'll be famous!"

"Well, I guess maybe I can accommodate you," he said. And he leaned way back in his rocker.

CHAPTER SEVEN
RED MEETS PAUL BUNYAN

Now, after Red and Tom'd spent a good while sorting things out, they—

Suddenly I heard a crow loud enough to raise the flag. "Now I've done it," said the farmer.

The crowing got louder, and the front door opened behind me. I turned around, and I couldn't believe my eyes. There he was, little as life: Rhode Island Red!

Oh, he was wearing bifocals and a hearing aid, and he walked with a cane, and his face was wrinklier than a petrified raisin, but there was no mistaking those carrot-colored locks. He walked over and kicked the farmer in the shins.

"I told you, Farmer Hockenbrocker!" Red shouted angrily. "Don't you ever tell that story!"

"Why in the world not?" I asked.

"Because it's *my* story, that's why not," Red said belligerently, limping up to my big toe. "A man's got to save something for his memoirs."

"I see your point."

"My trouble is—typing. Hard enough to set down my memoirs when I can't read or write, without having to dance the turkey trot all over a mess of machinery."

"Maybe I could lend a hand," I offered.

"Maybe you could at that," he said. We bargained for about an hour over how much I should get paid for my services and who'd supply the paper and this and that and a few other things, and somewhere in there I must've dozed off.

The sun was shining bright as diamonds and sparkling on the dew by the time I woke up, though my head felt like it'd grown feathers on the inside. I noticed something penciled on my shirt cuff: "Write it up good now. Got to do my chores. Hockenbrocker."

I shook some of the cobwebs from my brain and hid the rest of 'em under my Stetson. I picked up my stack of old newspapers with scribbling in the margins and took them out to my car.

Did I really meet Rhode Island Red? Did I really talk with the greatest little hero America has ever known, or was it the rainwater talking? The question kept preying on my mind as I put the car in gear and started down the road.

Farmer Hockenbrocker was tending his tomato patch as I drove past. As he waved good-bye, he pointed toward the top of the henhouse.

I looked up: It was too bright to tell for sure, but I thought I could make out a tiny figure of a man riding the weathercock. I do know for certain I heard the loudest *Cock-a-doodle-doo!* in the history of chickendom come at me from that very spot. And that's no cock and bull, friend.